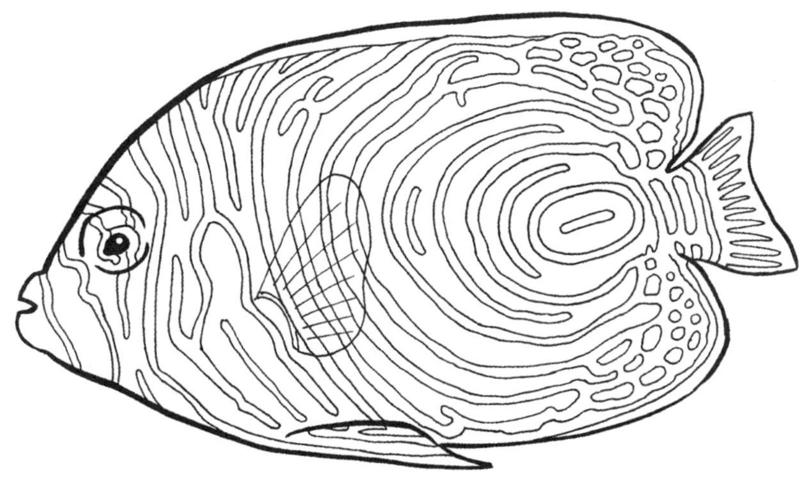

Australian Fishes Colour and Learn

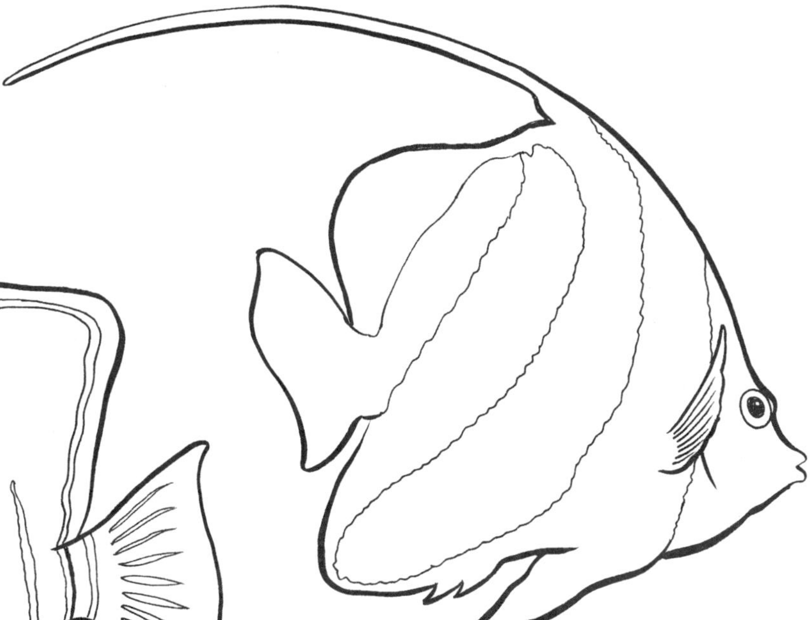

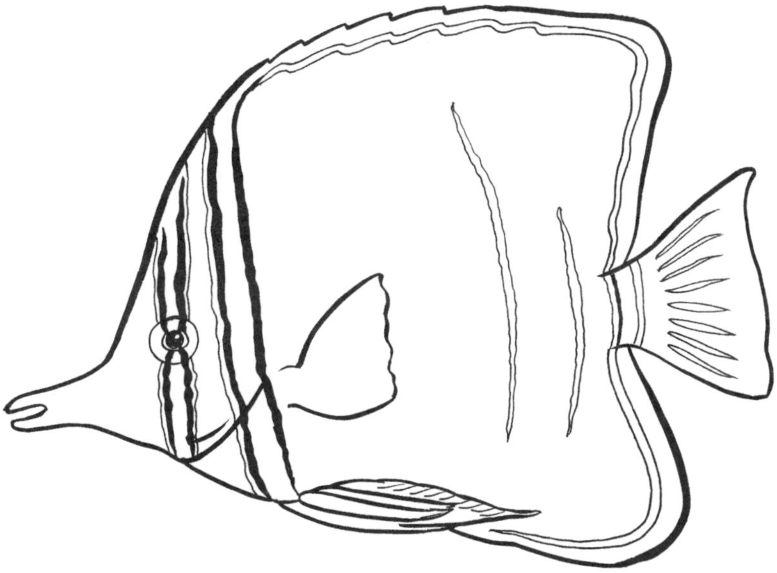

young reed

The world's longest fish, this huge shark often grows to about twelve metres long – that's the same as SEVEN adult humans laying head to toe! These gentle giants are not at all dangerous – they filter seawater to feed on tiny animals such as plankton.

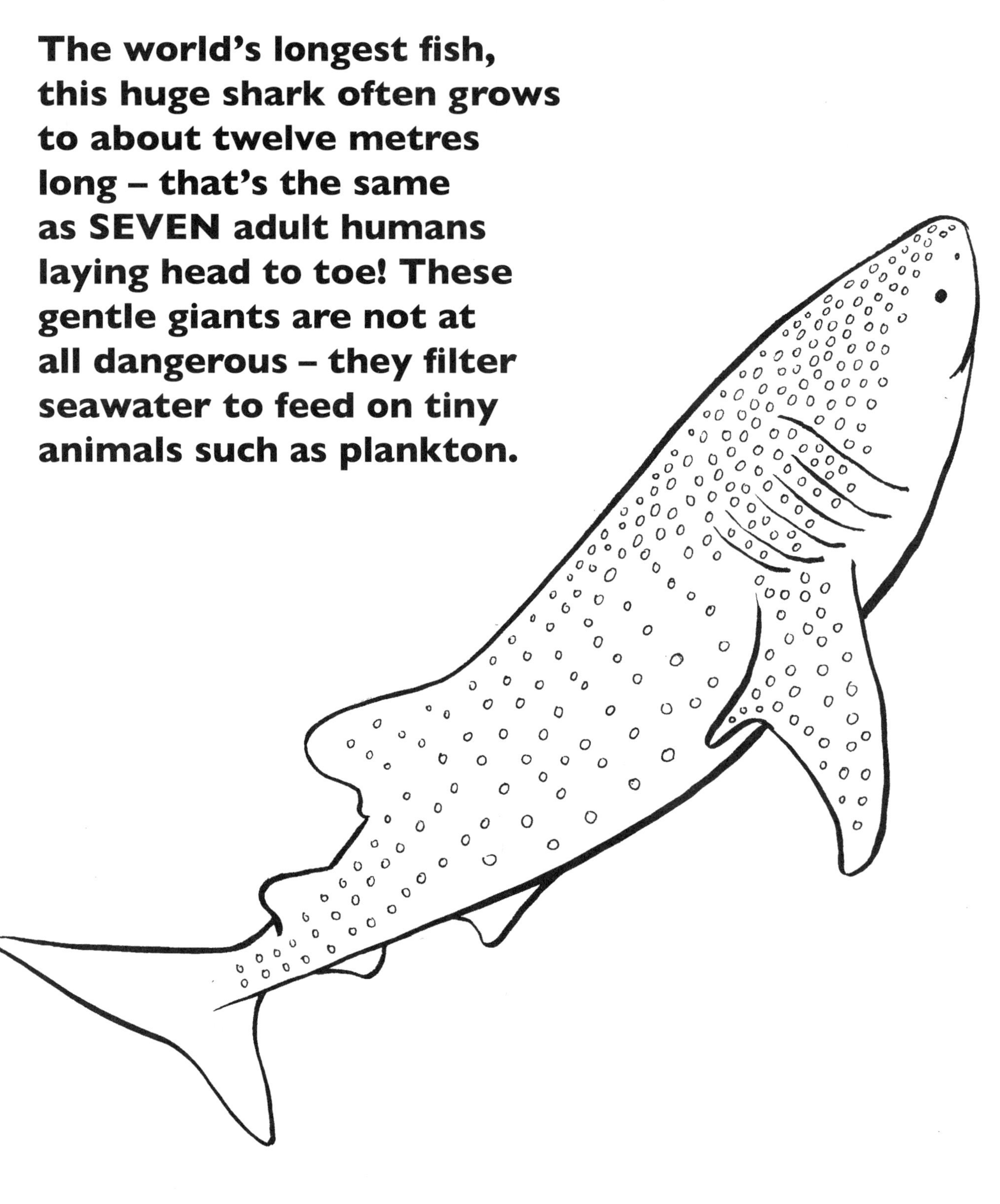

Whale Shark

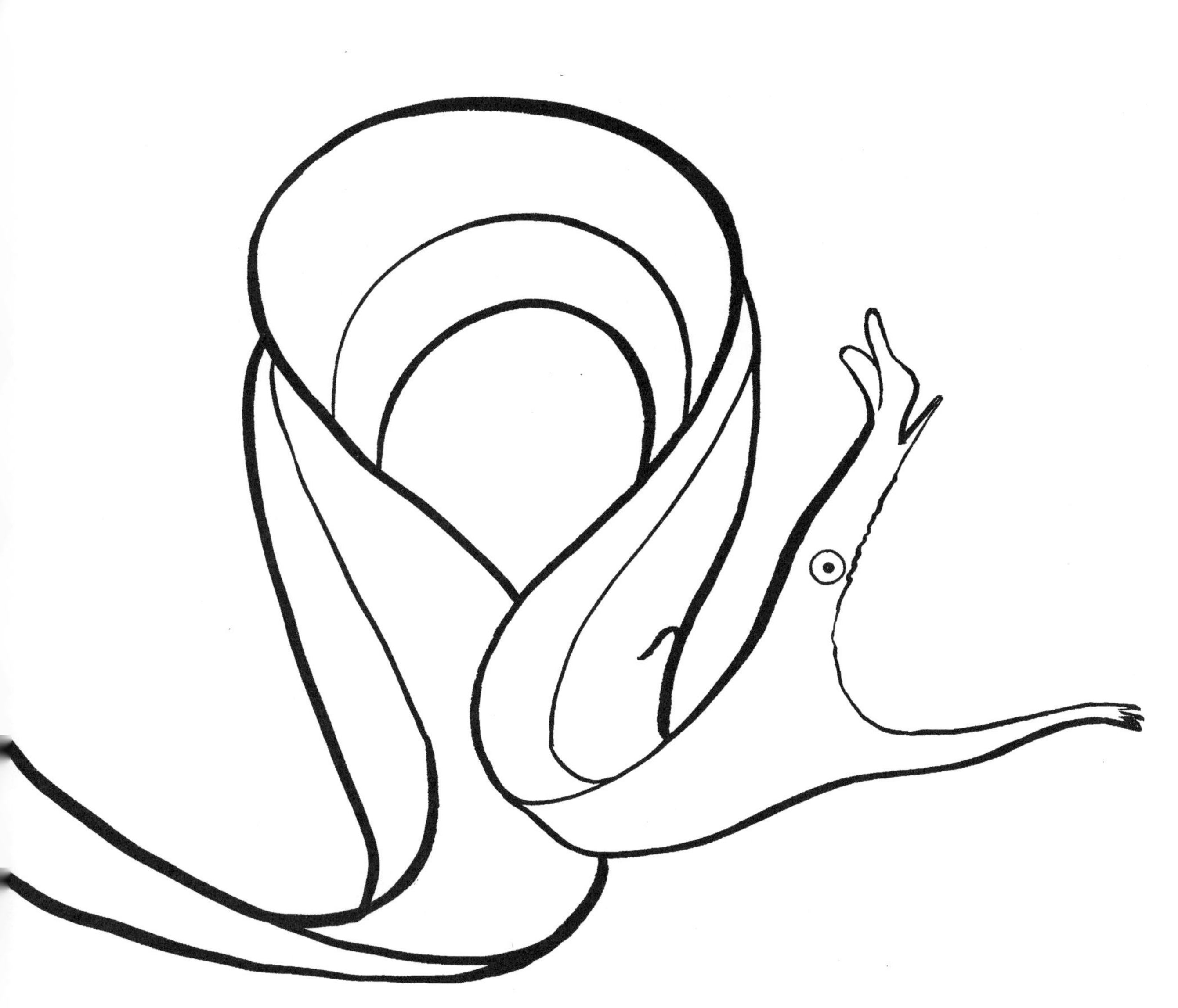

The head of this colourful fish looks a bit like a dragon's. They live on reefs off northern Australia and in the Pacific Ocean and can bite to protect themselves if threatened. Amazingly, males can change into females.

Ribbon Eel

Not the prettiest fish in the ocean, this species is remarkable nonetheless. Its fins are a bit like legs and it can use them for moving around the reef. Its skin can change colour, to help with camouflage when trying to get closer to catch its prey.

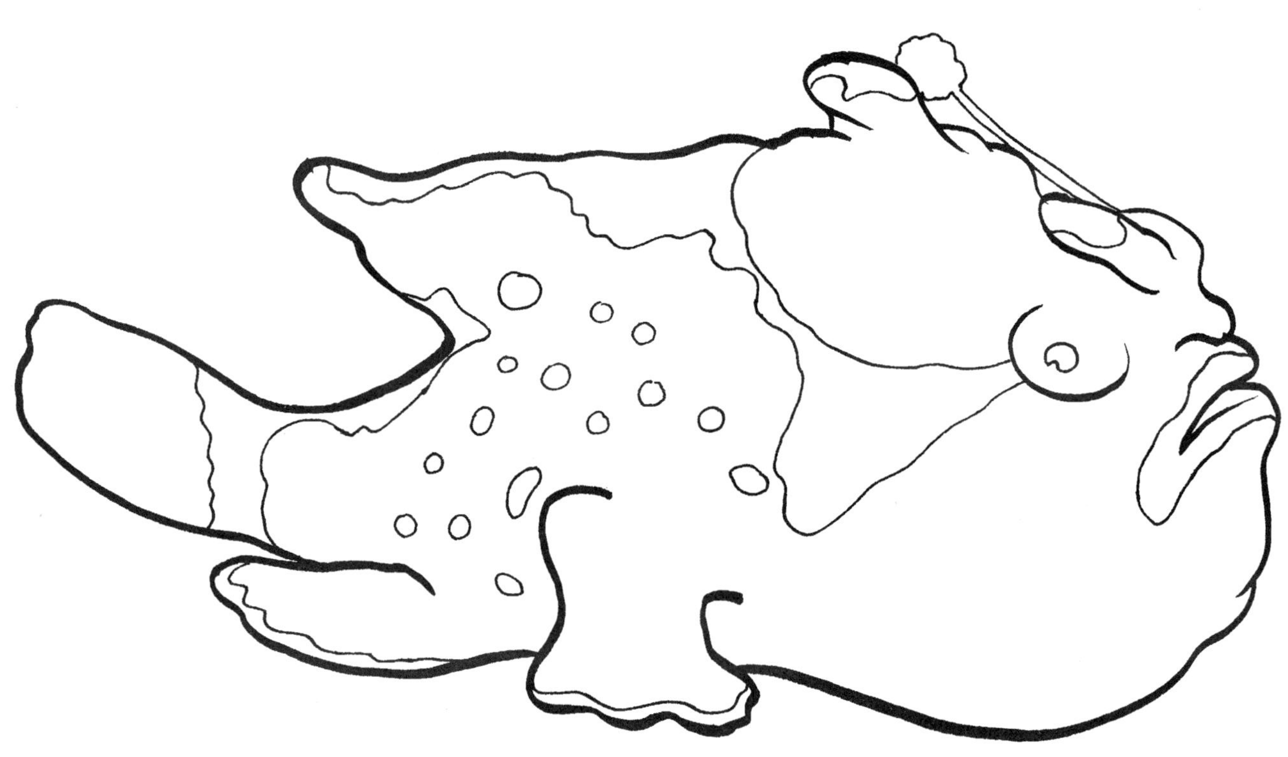

Warty Anglerfish

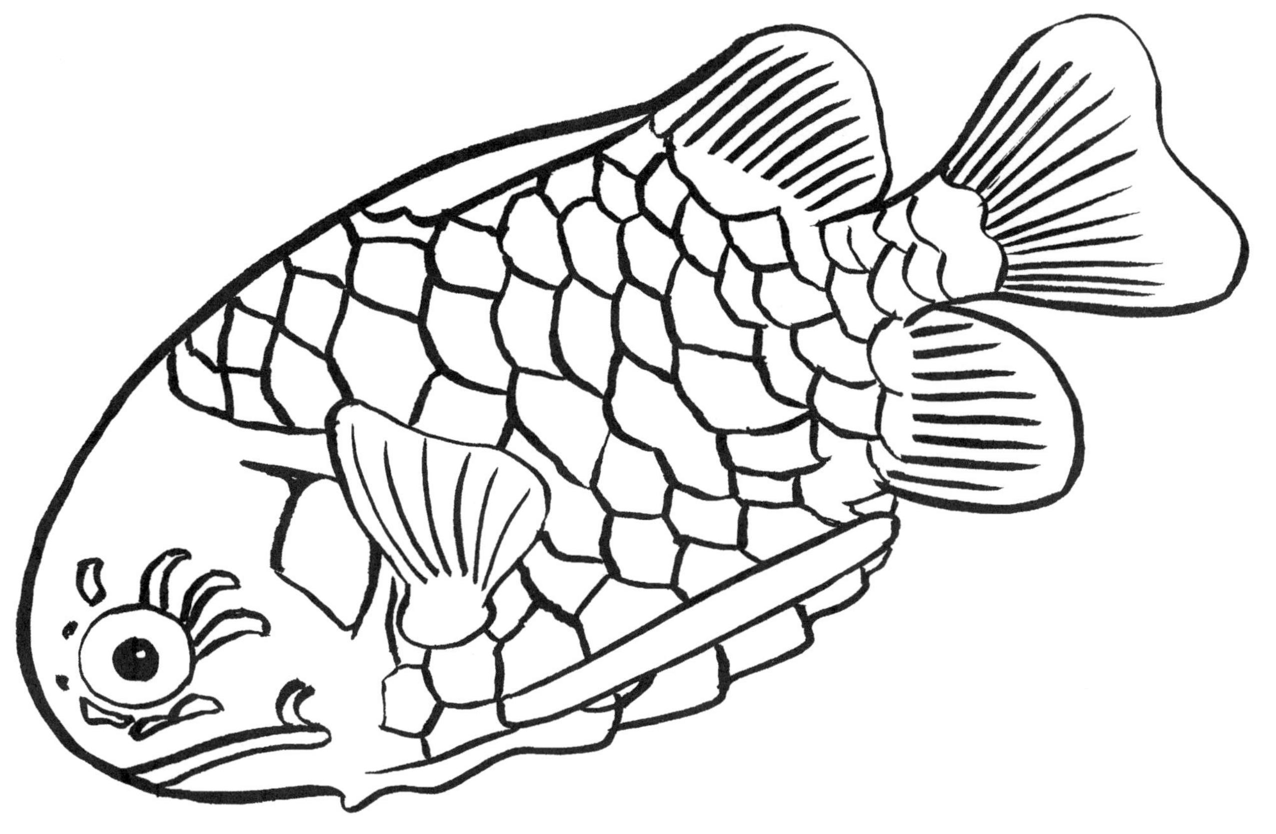

The amazing pattern of this species has led to the name pineapplefish, and also the alternative name 'pinecone fish'. The large scales act like a suit of armour and afford excellent protection against predators.

Australian Pineapplefish

A member of the seahorse family, this incredible fish takes camouflage to extremes and its fins look exactly like pieces of seaweed. It lives only along the south coast of Australia and can be very tricky to spot.

Leafy Seadragon

This beautiful-looking fish protects itself from being eaten with an array of poisonous spines. It lives in shallow waters and on reefs and in recent years has spread around the world. A female can lay up to 30,000 eggs in a season.

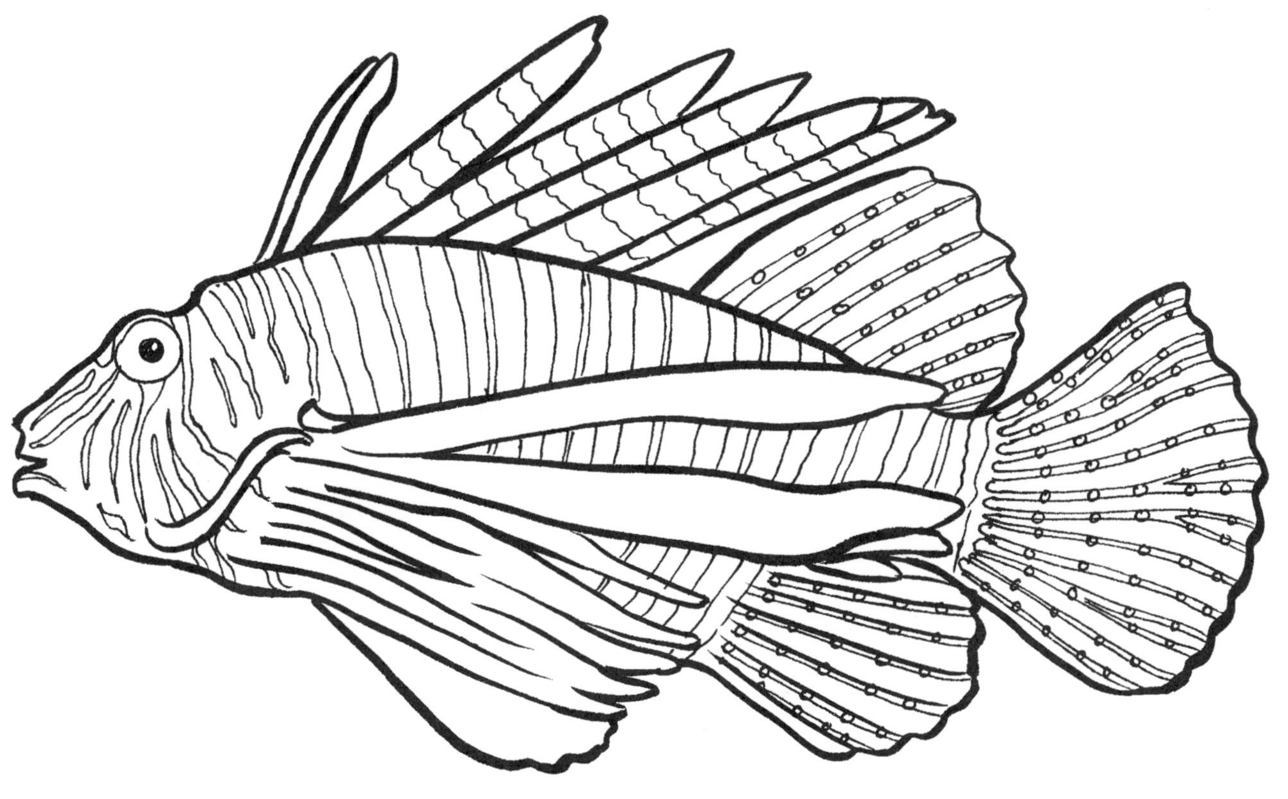

Common Lionfish

These amazing giants of the reefs can grow to two metres in length and weigh as much as 110kg – that's about the same as a refrigerator! Also known as Potato Groupers, they are covered in potato-shaped spots and can produce a loud grumbling noise that sometimes frightens divers.

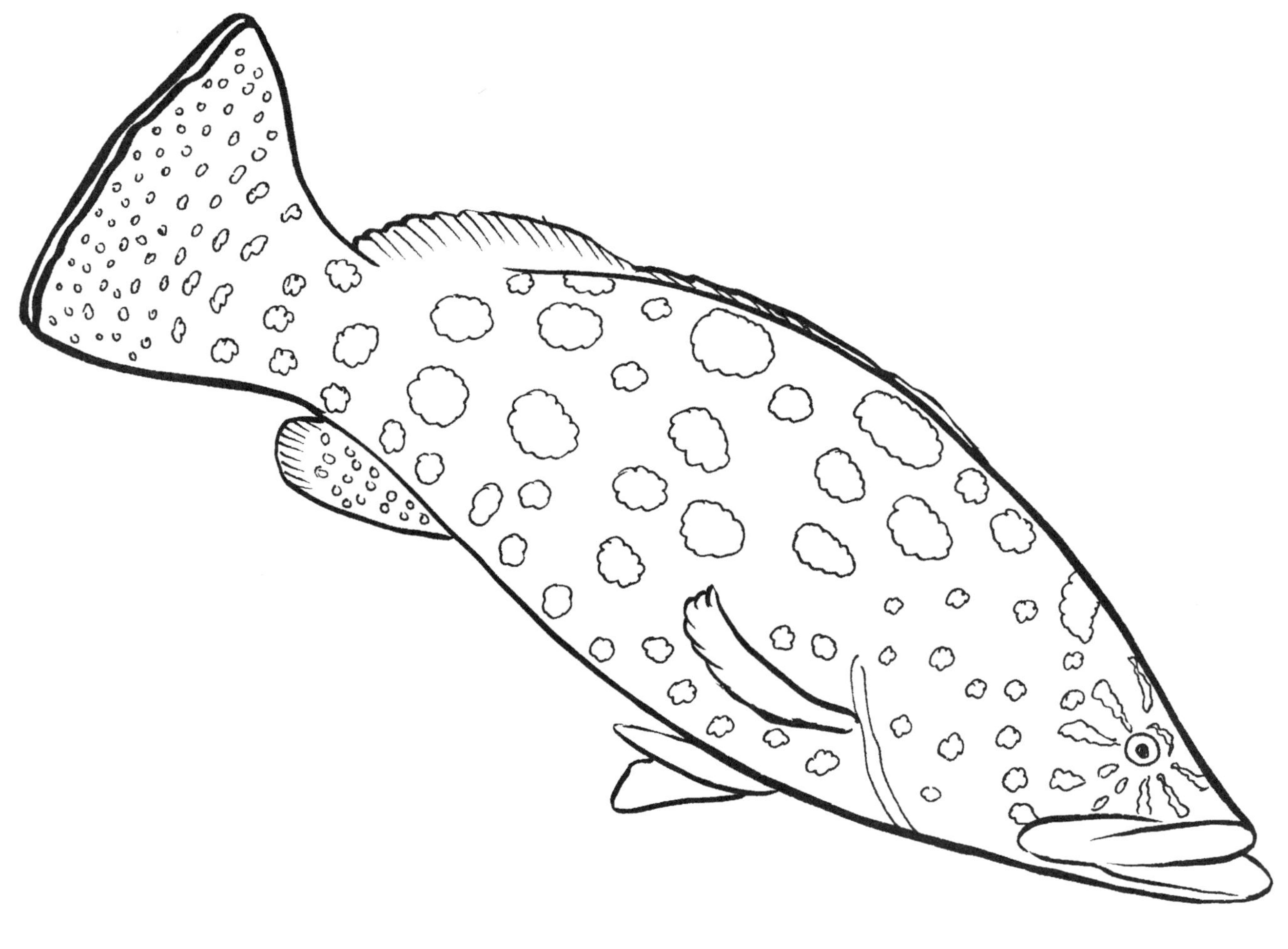

Potato Rockcod

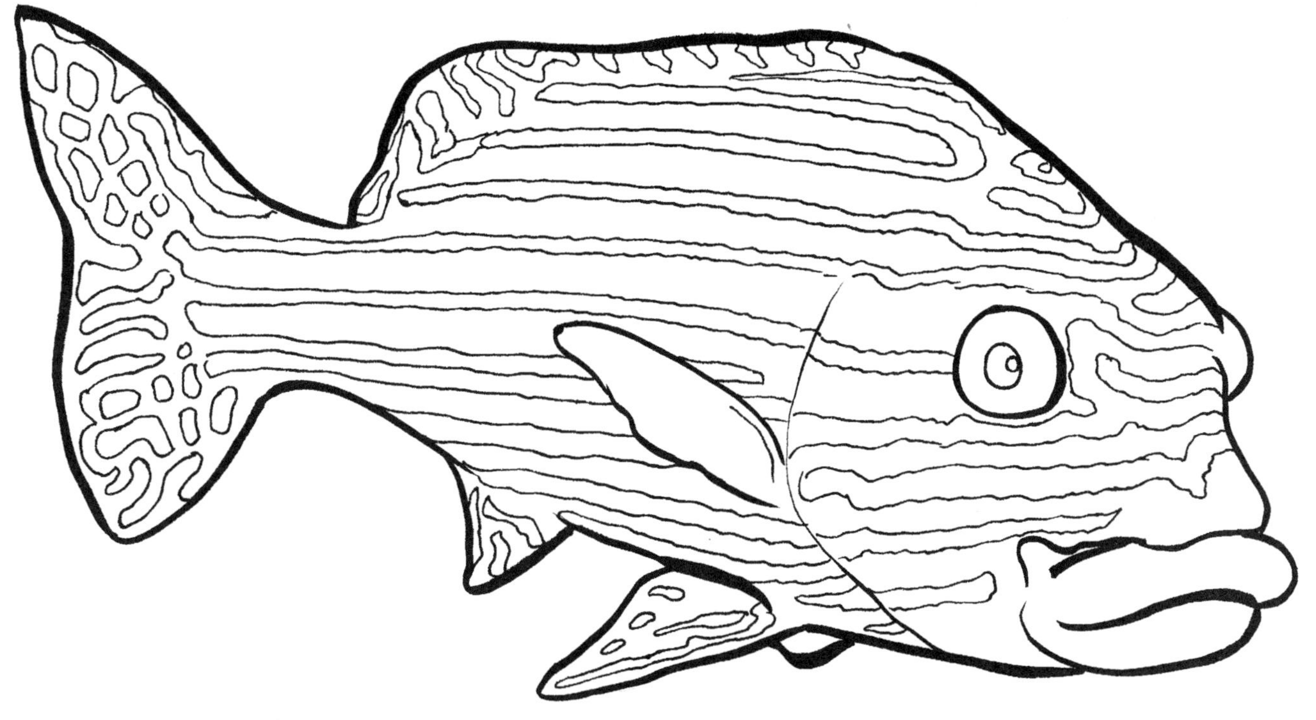

Also known as 'blubberlips'. With brilliant yellow and blue colours, a striped body and spotted fins and tail, this eye-catching species can be found on northern reefs. The young look completely different to the adults – they are orange-brown with large white blotches.

Oriental Sweetlips

Often seen in large schools, keeping company with other fish species. Named after the long spine which extends behind the dorsal fin. Seen around reefs off the east and west coasts of Australia.

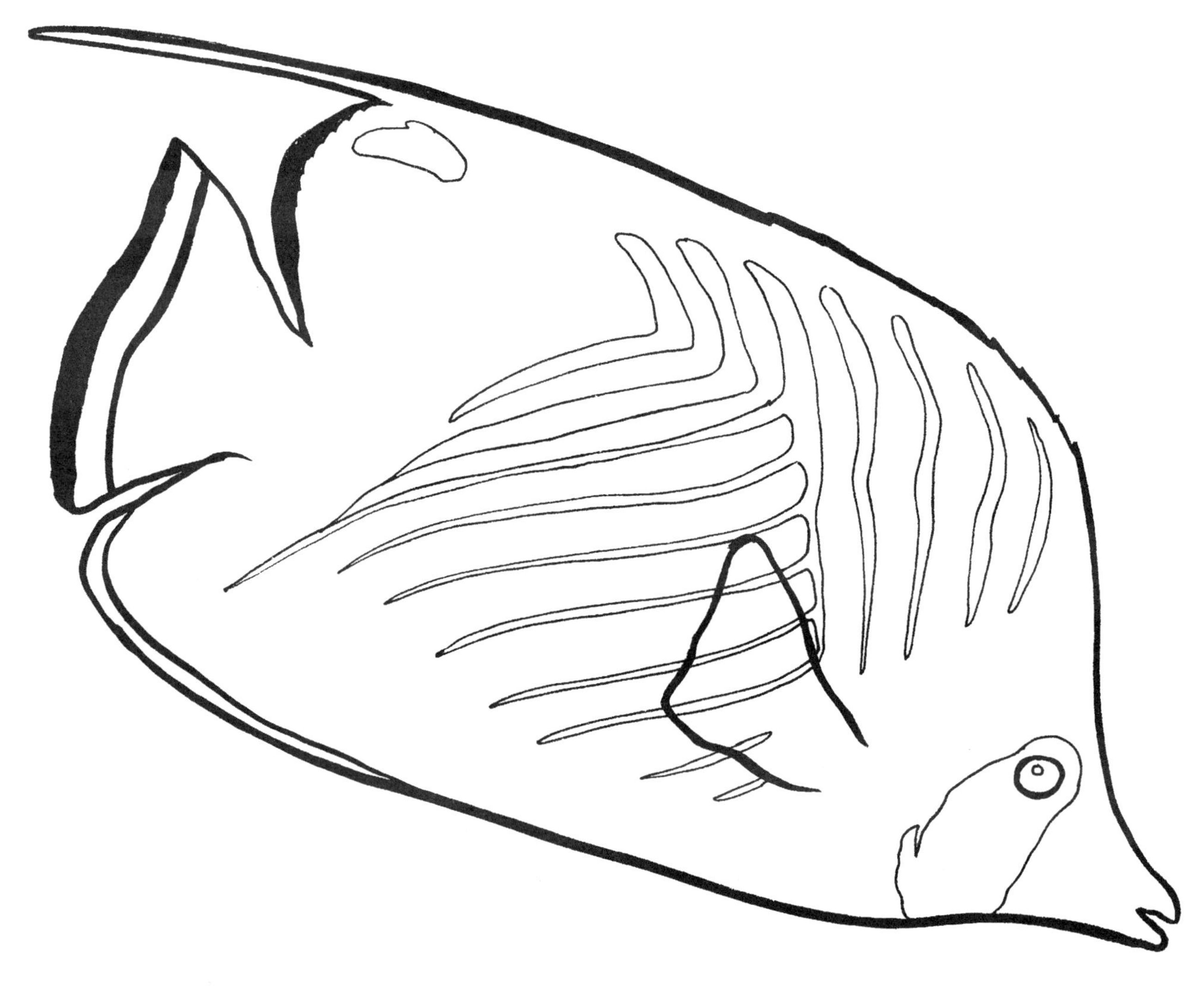

Threadfin Butterflyfish

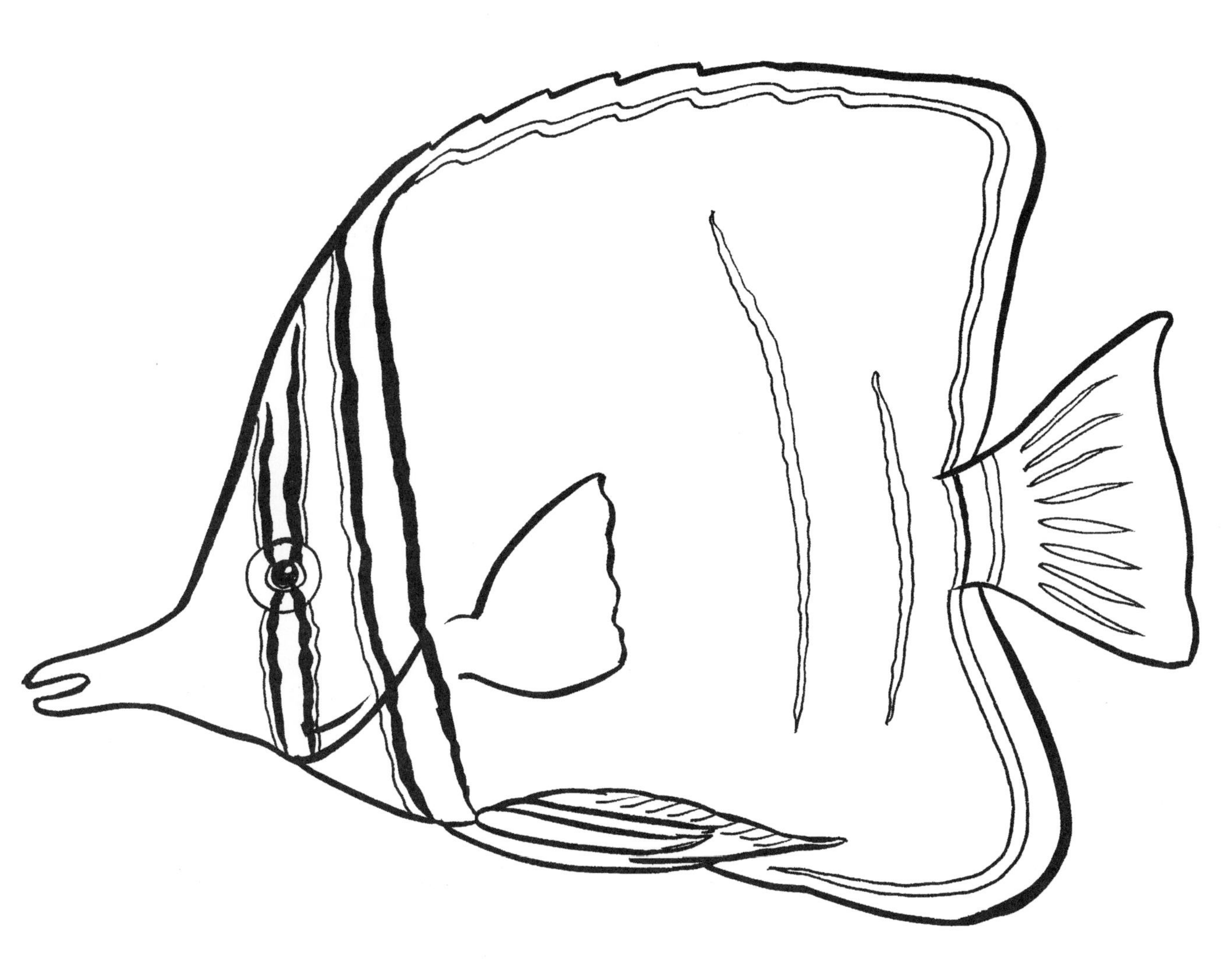

This species is endemic to seas around northern Australia, which means that it occurs nowhere else in the world. The long 'beak' is used for nibbling at prey such as tubeworms and clams. Juveniles have four orange bands, adults only two.

Margined Coralfish

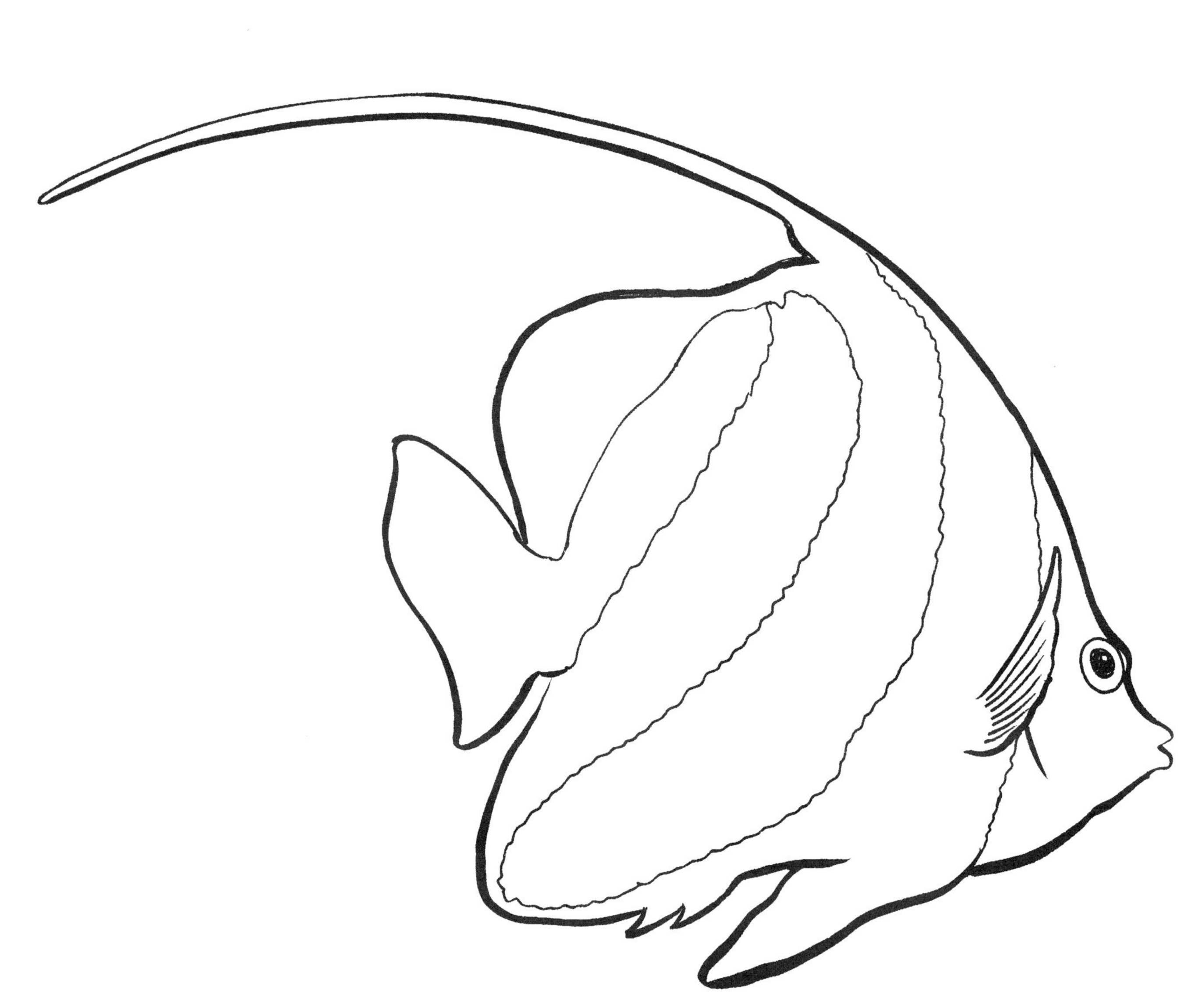

With a very long banner-like dorsal fin, this beautiful fish grows up to 25cm long and is sometimes kept as a pet. In the wild it occurs in seas all around Australia except off the south coast.

Longfin Bannerfish

The young of this species (pictured) looks completely different to the adult with its pattern of concentric blue rings resembling those of a cut tree trunk. In contrast the adult is boldly striped yellow and blue and looks a little bit like an Oriental Sweetlips.

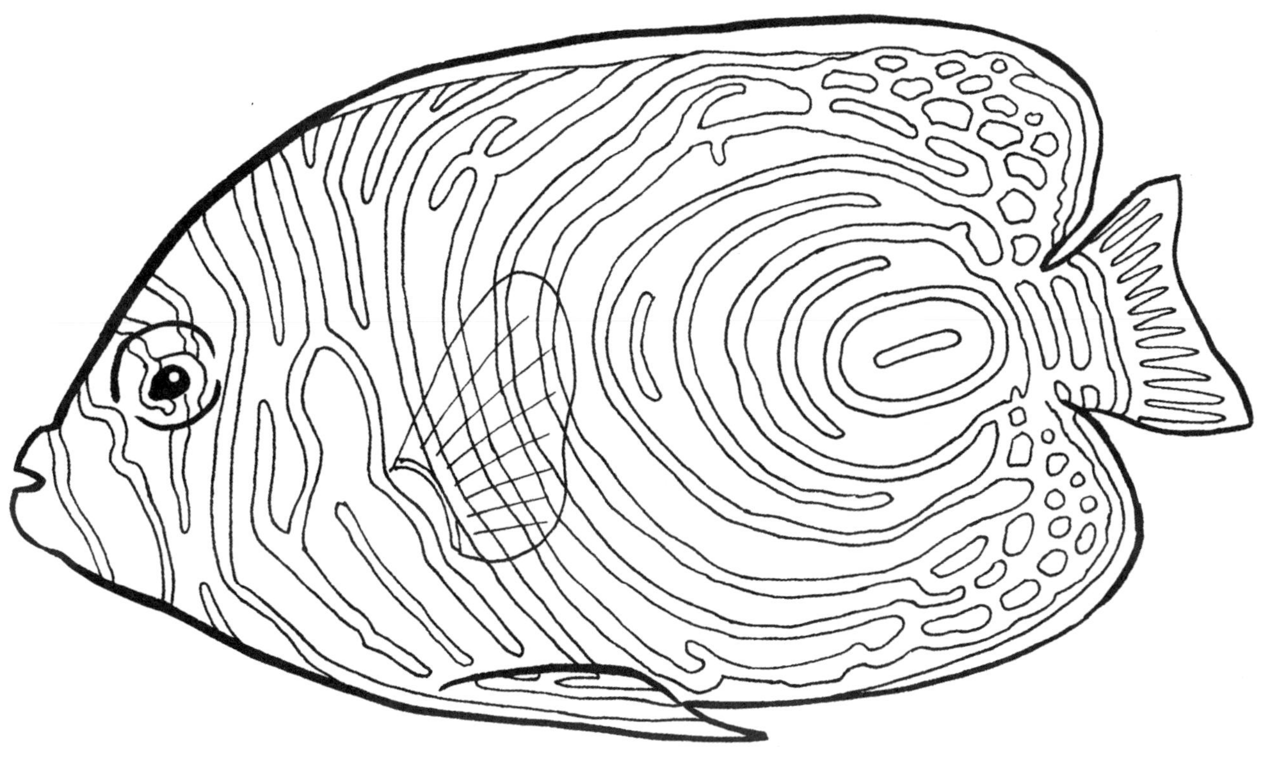

Emperor Angelfish

It's easy to see why these beautiful medium-sized sharks are so named, thanks to the adult's covering of black spots on a yellowish background. They are also known as Zebra Sharks because the young have a completely different pattern of black and white stripes.

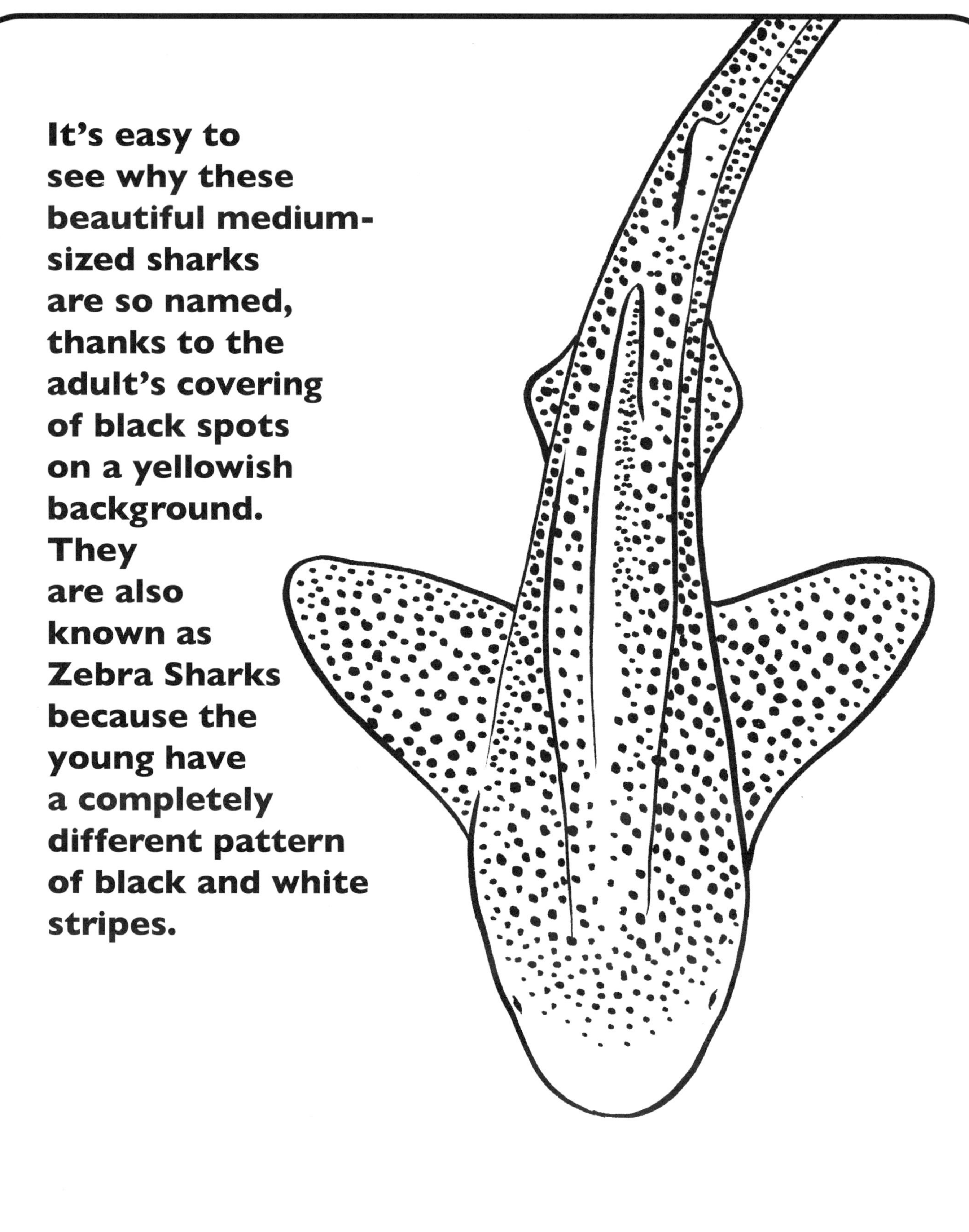

Leopard Shark

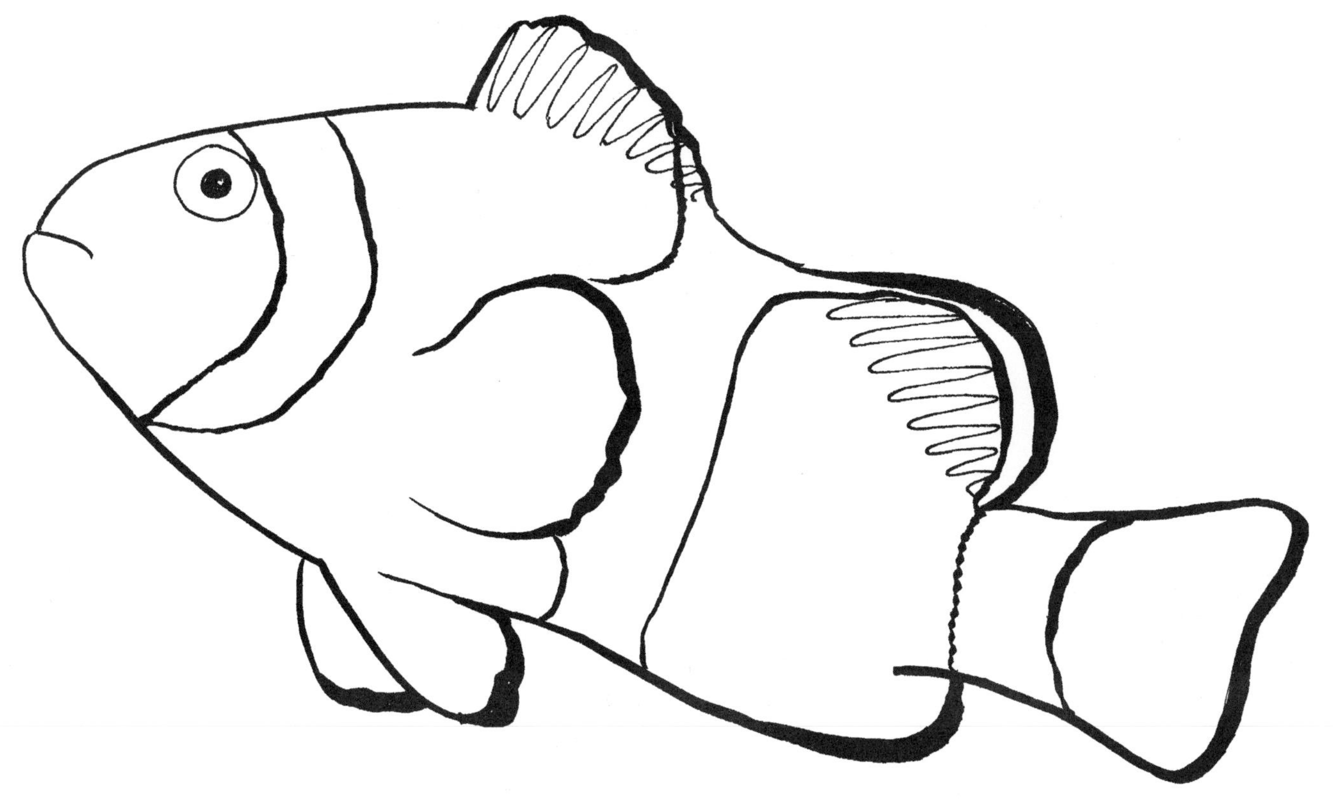

One of more than ten similar species that occur around Australia which have been made famous by the animated character 'Nemo' in Disney films. Also known as 'clownfish', they can live within sea anemones without being stung by the tentacles, while males can change into females.

Western Clown Anemonefish

These beautiful small fish are very variable in colour and pattern. When sleeping they burrow into sand for protection. Found off the coasts of northern Australia, those in the Indian Ocean may be a different species to the ones in the Pacific – further study is required!

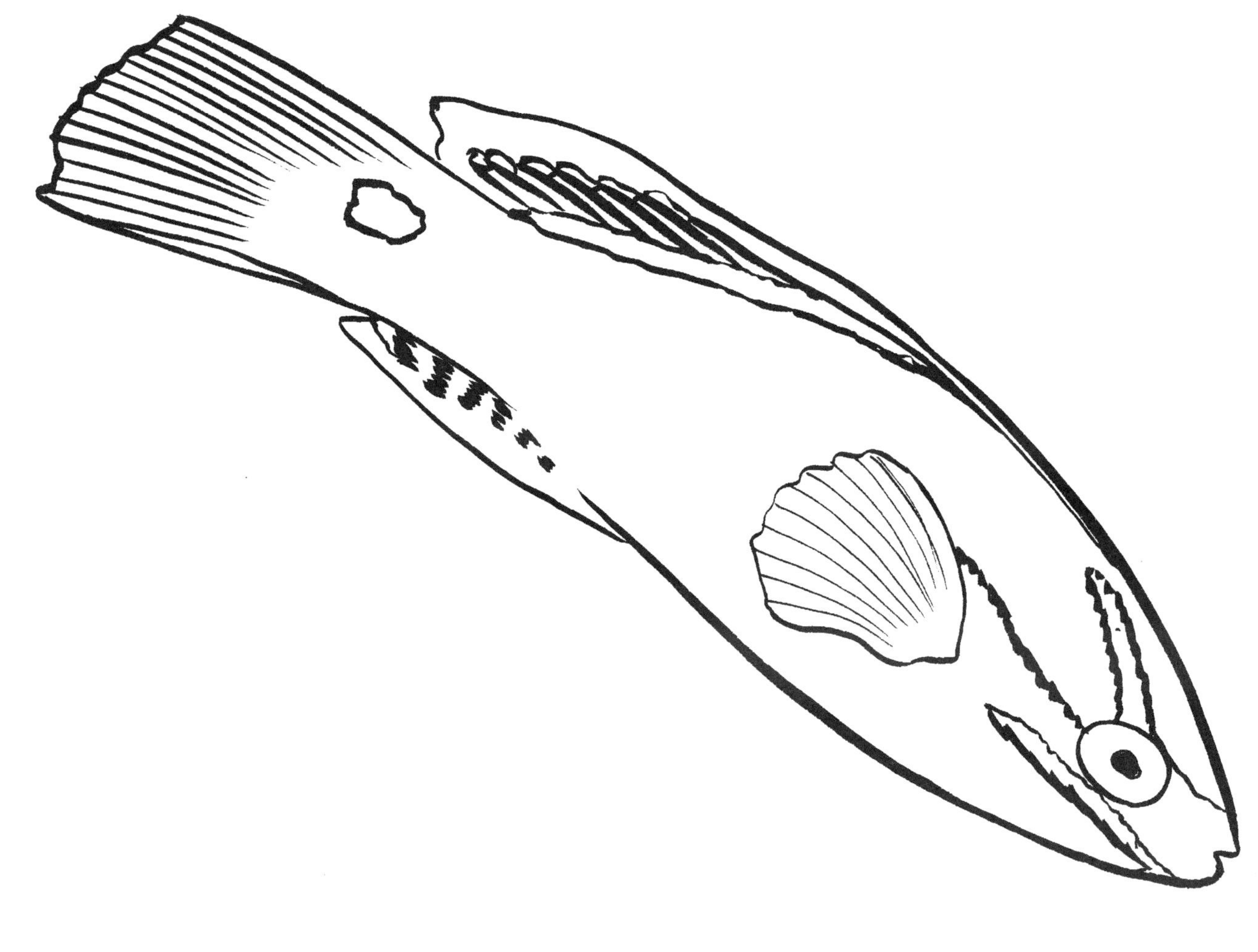

Exquisite Wrasse

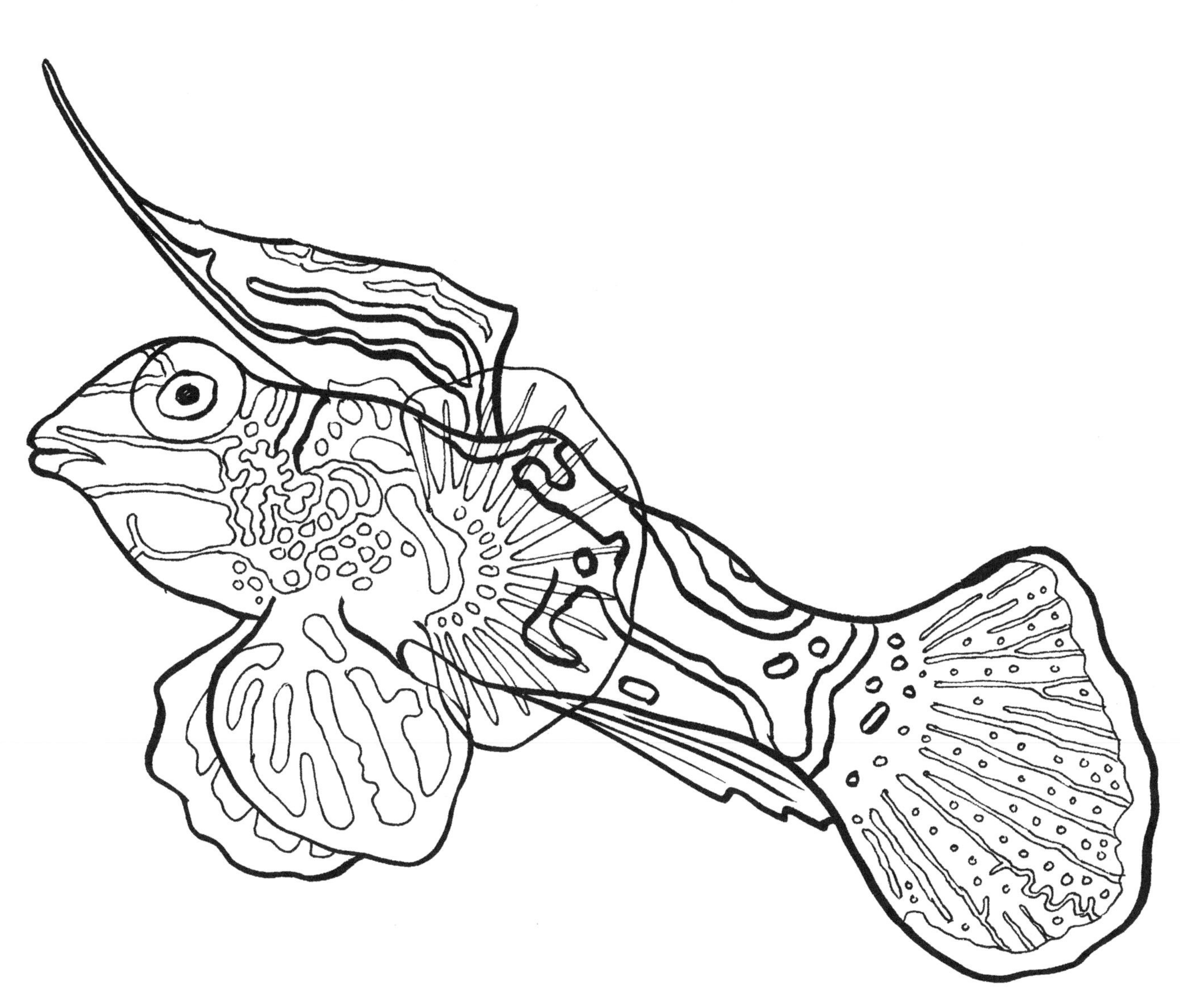

It is hard to believe that so many colours and patterns can be crammed on to one 7cm-long fish. Found in waters off northern Australia, the Mandarinfish is unusual because it does not have scales and it performs an amazing 'dance' during the breeding season.

Mandarinfish

Only the youngsters of this species are bright yellow – older fish are pale brown or blue. If threatened the boxfish releases a cloud of toxins that can kill other fish that are nearby, although the chemicals can also be a danger to the boxfish itself!

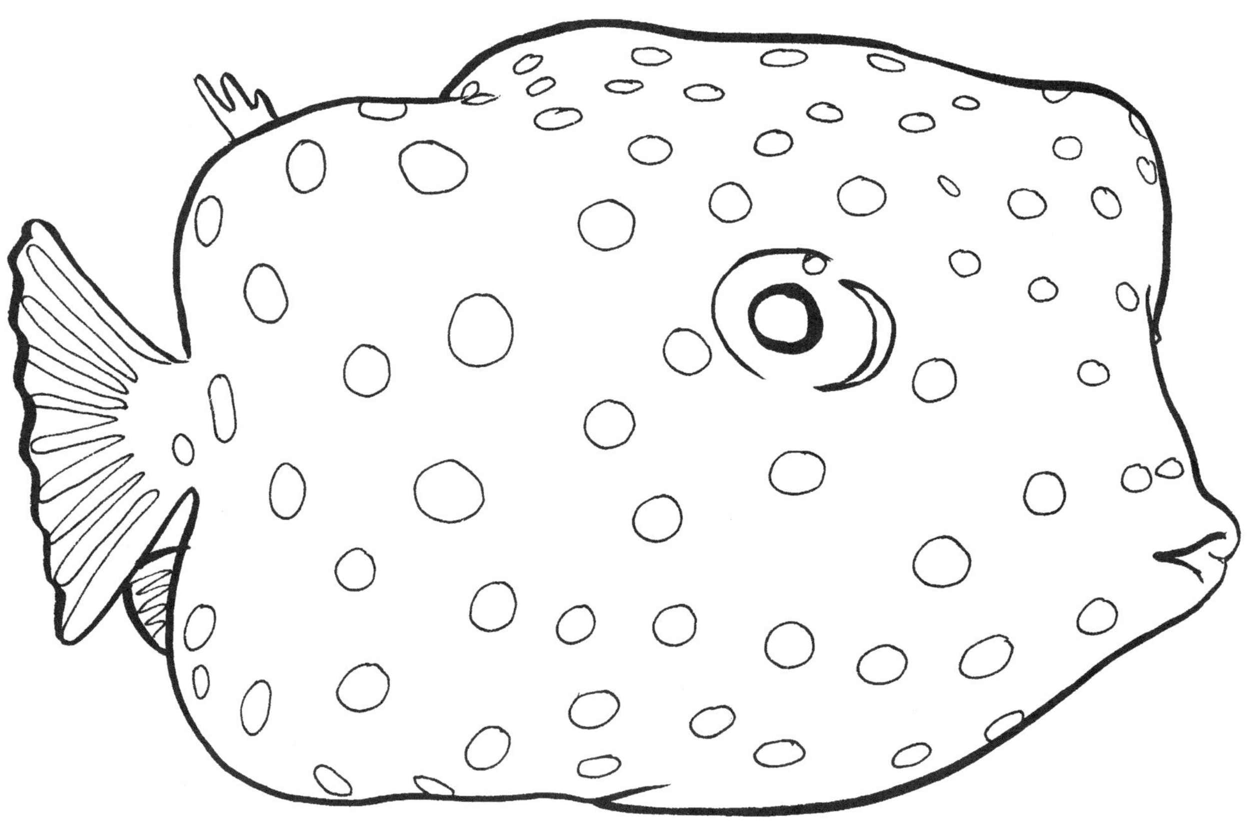

Yellow Boxfish

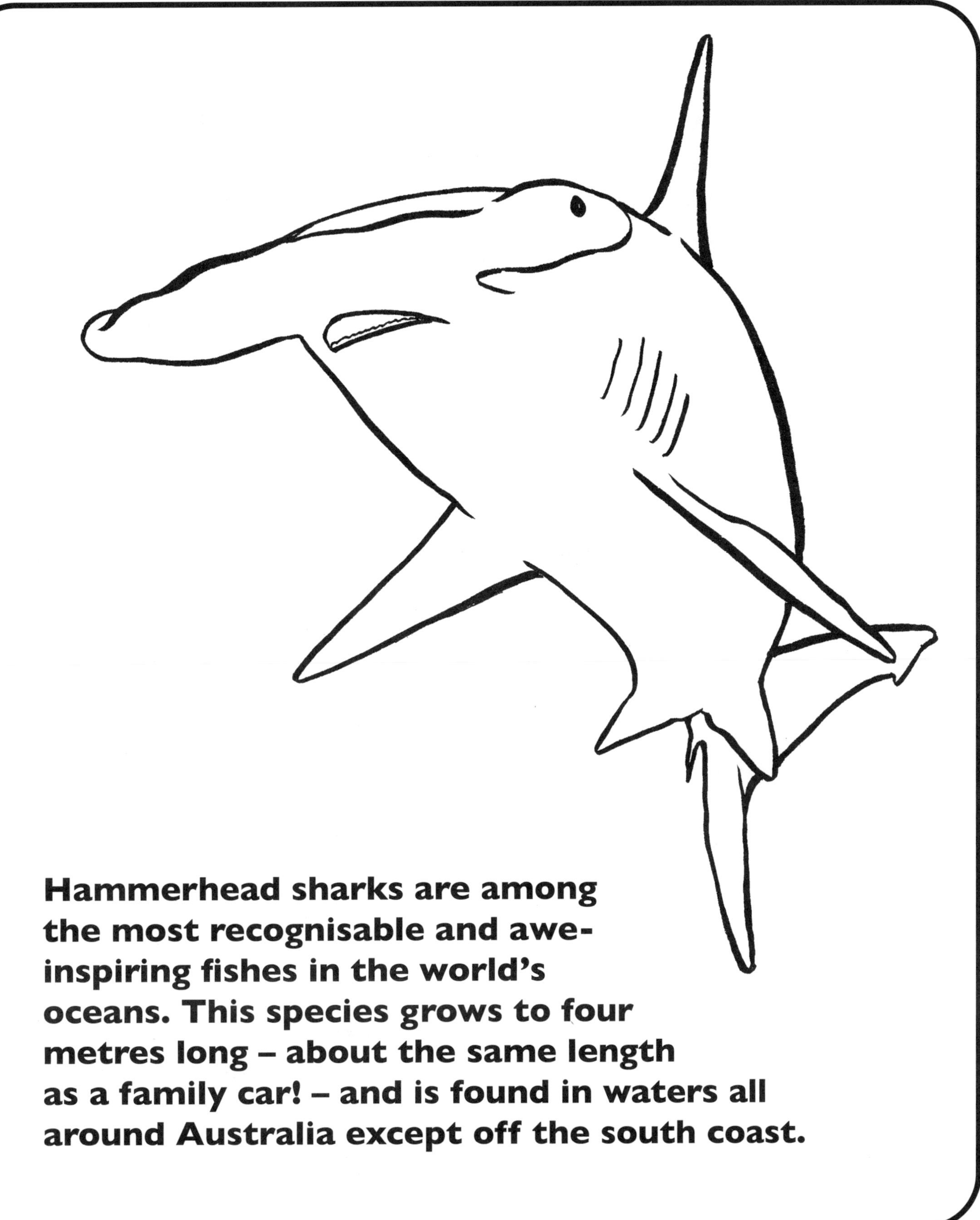

Hammerhead sharks are among the most recognisable and awe-inspiring fishes in the world's oceans. This species grows to four metres long – about the same length as a family car! – and is found in waters all around Australia except off the south coast.

Scalloped Hammerhead

A distinctive blue and black fish with a bright yellow tail that is found on reefs along the east coast of Australia. It has sharp spines on its tail which help to protect it from predators.

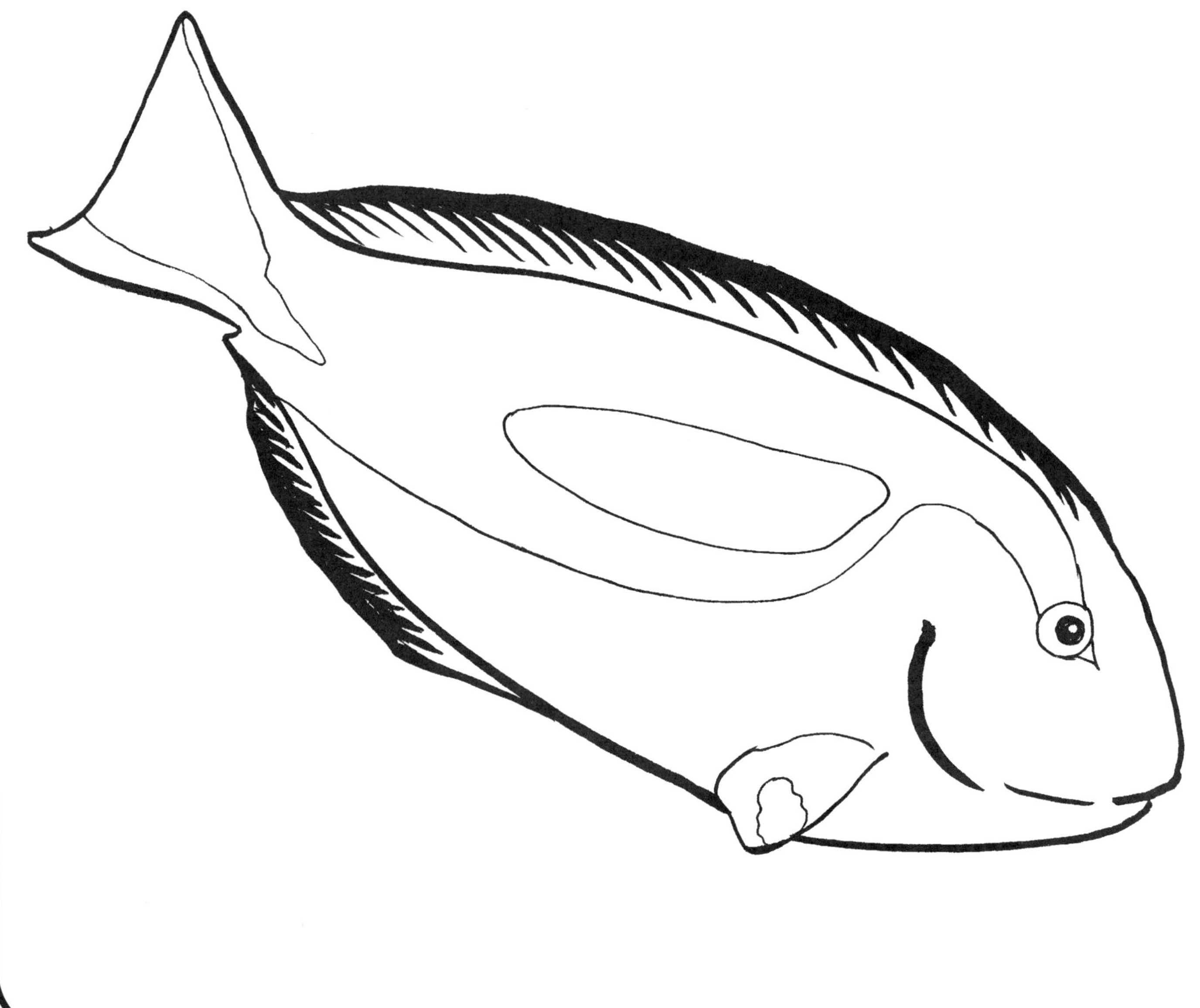

Blue Tang

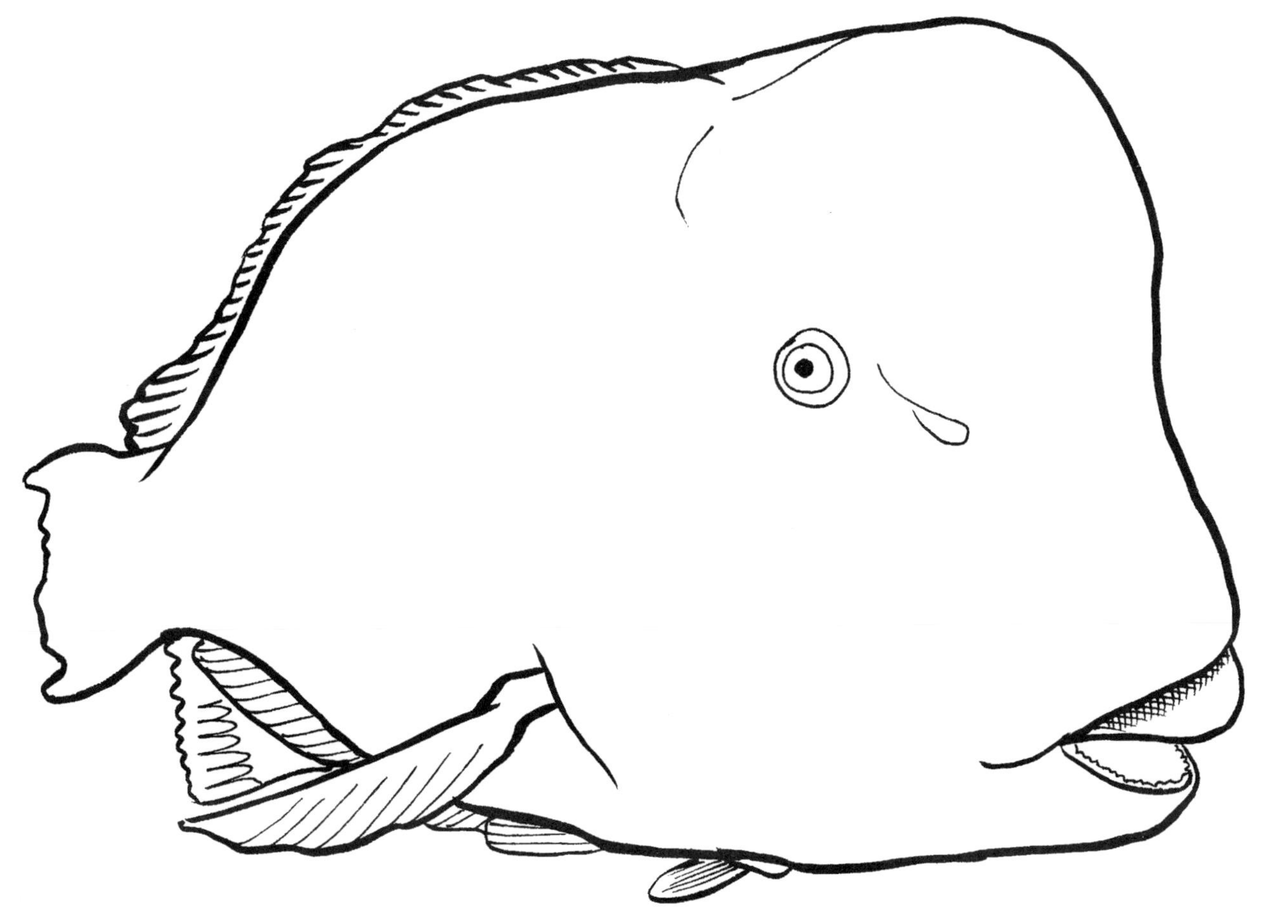

The bump on the head is used to help break off pieces of coral and algae when feeding. The fish needs to continually regrow its teeth due to this diet, and it poops out any hard pieces of coral as sand.

Bumphead Parrotfish

A distinctive bright orange-yellow fish with a black and white head. It grows up to 25cm long, lives on coral reefs in tropical waters and protects itself from danger with the help of a row of venomous spines along its dorsal fin.

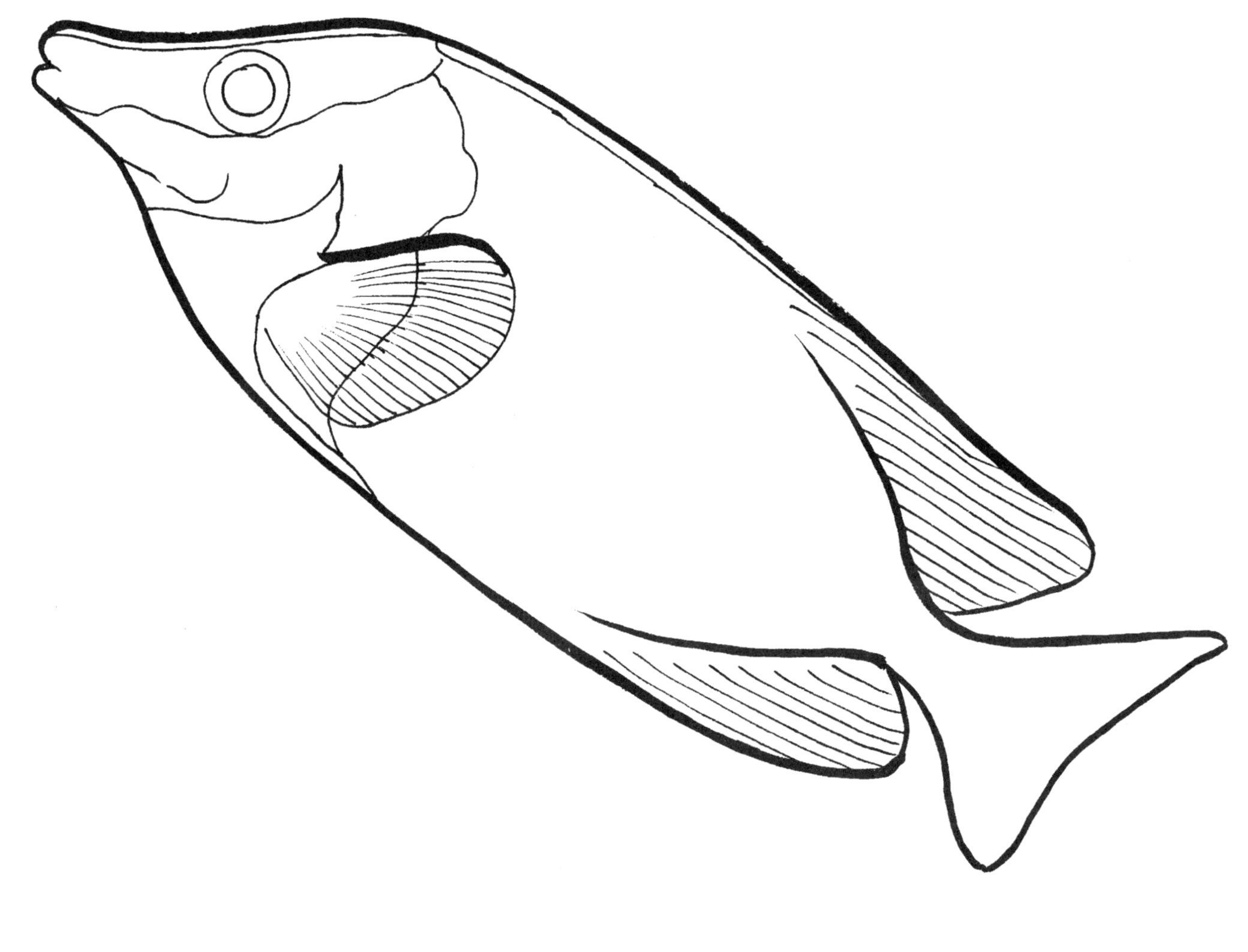

Foxface Rabbitfish

One of a number of similar demoiselle species, this small fish grows to 9cm and is found on reefs off northern Australia. Its body is a beautiful iridescent turquoise-blue with black spots and the male has an orange-red tail.

Blue Demoiselle

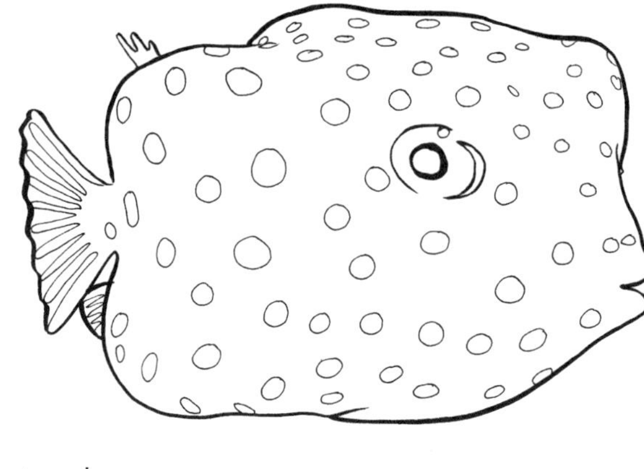

Published in 2023 by Reed New Holland Publishers
Sydney

Level 1, 178 Fox Valley Road, Wahroonga, NSW 2076, Australia

newhollandpublishers.com

A record of this book is held at the National Library of Australia.

ISBN 978 1 92158 063 5

Managing Director: Fiona Schultz
Publisher and Project Editor: Simon Papps
Designer and illustrator: Andrew Davies
Production Director: Arlene Gippert
Printed in China

10 9 8 7 6 5 4 3 2 1

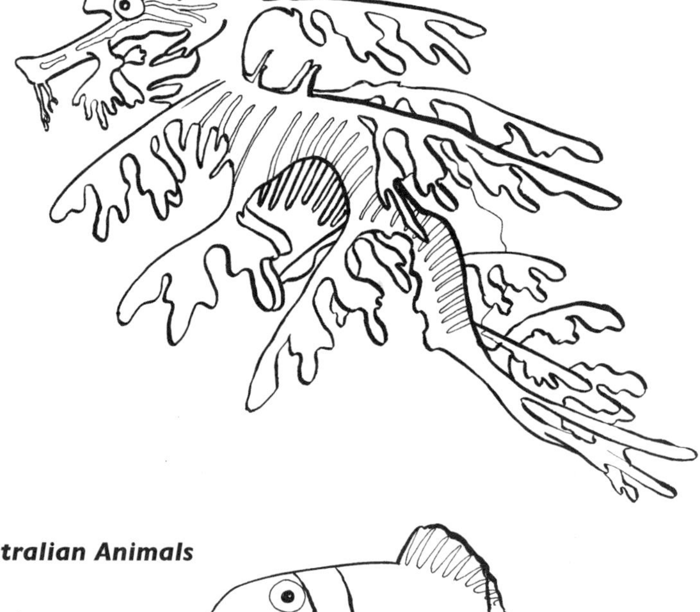